AMER-
-I CAN
MUSIC
CHRIS
MARTIN

Also by Chris Martin

American Music (isabel lettres, 2005)

The Day Reagan Died (isabel lettres, 2004)

Vermontana (Angry Dog Midget Editions, 2003)

Gross Exaggerations, with kari edwards (xPress(ed), 2002)

The Smallish Lever (Bench Press, 2002)

Regarding the Uncertain Distinction Between Art & Hat
    (Bench Press, 2001)

Flex (Bench Press, 2001)

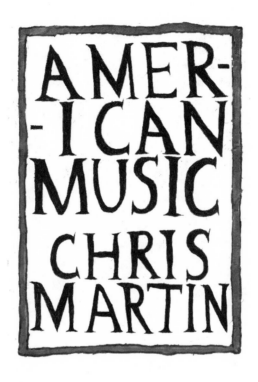

AMER-
-ICAN
MUSIC
CHRIS
MARTIN

COPPER CANYON PRESS

Port Townsend, Washington

Cover art: Simon Evans, *Untitled*, 2005. Collage, tape and clothing lint, 11 x 17 inches.

Copper Canyon Press is in residence at Fort Worden State Park in Port Townsend, Washington, under the auspices of Centrum. Centrum is a gathering place for artists and creative thinkers from around the world, students of all ages and backgrounds, and audiences seeking extraordinary cultural enrichment.

Earlier versions of some of these poems appeared in a chapbook under the same name from the esteemed isabel lettres.

LIBRARY OF CONGRESS CATALOGING-IN-PUBLICATION DATA

Martin, Chris, 1977 Aug. 11–
  American music / Chris Martin.
      p. cm.
  ISBN 978-1-55659-266-9 (alk. paper)
  1. Cities and towns—Poetry. 2. United States—Social conditions—Poetry. I. Title.

  PS3613.A77785A84 2007
  811'.6–dc22

                                        2007020184

1 2 3 4 5 6 7 8 9 0 FIRST PRINTING

COPPER CANYON PRESS
Post Office Box 271
Port Townsend, Washington 98368
www.coppercanyonpress.org

*The world's furious
song flows through my
costume*

Ted Berrigan

Plagiarism is necessary

Guy Debord

Contents

AMERICAN MUSIC

Jokes for Strangers

All twenty-first-century
Day long I compose these jokes
For myself and strangers

For the cats also, stuck
As they are in the airshaft
As am I, breath

Meandering through its conspiratorial
Orbits, circling the eyes
Which goggle sprightly, peering

Into the habitual arrangements and I
Am a joke too sometimes
The way a horse burns down

To bridle and the mind lingers
On cake, we are all plastic
Miniatures trembling amid the acoustics

Electrified, my sword bending like
A cactus, the ruthless wind
Upon it, I thought it terribly

Important to bed
A woman of learning
To feel *The Sonnets*

And fill the empty drawer
A bus stampedes
Down Ninth Street, cauterizing

Certain possibilities of space
I can't tell you
How much it means to lose even

An unwanted quantity
Of variousness, as perhaps
All my decisions end

With hard looks into the oily distance
Of urban mirage, fuck
Not getting a job, I've got kids

To learn, Palestinian
Kids, Italian kids, kids like myself wrung
Whiter each genealogical turn and

Who's looking out for us? The president? Even
Cars crossing the street are doomed
To simple sympathizing over the inglorious

Physics of contact, they are not human
And therefore have no problem
Staving off the delirium of hate, you have not

Died before, you are no
Perverted ghost lifting a skirt
With the empty pang

Of regret, you are not the resurrection of Giorgio
De Chirico, who died the year Denver
Lost its first Super Bowl, the year I was

Weaned and stamps cost an unlucky
Thirteen cents, which doesn't mean colonnades
Are any less haunted, mustachioed women

Rolling tremendous wheels of cheese
Along their claustrophobic geometries
I may have lost

My attention for Logic
But I see beautiful
Children circumventing cruelty

Nearly every day and it raises
The question—what have you done
Lately for the safety

Of our feelings? Have you
Offered your seat on a crowded
Downtown subway car

To a man in perfect physical health
Because he had tears in his eyes? Neither
Have I, not yet, but at least

I considered it in writing.

Trajectory of a Thief

It's simple, a life
Of eccentric guessing
You move

To California, one drunk
Night you climb
Every fence in the neighborhood

And no one shoots you
And fog washes
The church steeple

Bare, months
Pass, you sell your car
To a surfer, move

Again, America roils, a man
Walks into a bar and then drives
Into a tree, you move

Again, one love
Recedes and another beckons
Brightly, your roommate

Gets rich and it befits
Her, the sun
Struggles over your eastward

Facing sill and it never
Occurs to you
To wonder how

It's happening, it's simple
Yves Klein invents
A color and it kills him

You steal six hundred thousand
Hours from god and fear
Capture constantly, one wriggling

Dactyl amid the day's lapidary
Scansion, you carry on
Unreasonably and bloodless

The moon is a rock that salutes
You for it, you forgo
Certain dignities, others

Are thrust upon you, animals
Curve to your touch, a Brooklyn boy
With an unpronounceable name

Writes *Fire is tasty*
You imbecile, the leaves
In the trees in

The park ignite and you climb
The fire escape to the roof
To chart the buildings' unwavering

Ballet of windows, bullets
Are cocked nearby, the cops drink
Beer from Styrofoam

Cups on the street below
Ted takes you to Chinatown for turtle
Soup, each piece

Of its floating meat
Wholly disparate, the cherry
Blossoms arrive and then

Dissipate triumphantly
Like the sting
Of winter, cephalopods slowly

Adapt, an anonymous
Russian woman saves you
From falling on

The subway, the rooftop
Reads GODOT, the waitress
At the diner calls

You Professor, it's simple
The wind hits
Your lips and you're

Pleased, a deer hits
Your father's car and you're
Inconsolable, a family

Of skunks makes purchase
Beneath the floorboards
And the impending decision puzzles

You—the stink or
The killing it
Takes to rid yourself

Of it, of them, what else?

I Am No Proprioceptivist

Sometimes when nothing
Happens the world feels terribly
Sincere, the gloom

Unsettles, its heaving cape
Perforated by dazzling
Banalities, just to stare out the window

Conjures children to go out squealing
Over the half-obscured remains
Of a bird delicately sprouting from a snow

Bank or a man relieving
Himself into a trashcan delicately
Placed in the trash, it is too

Wondrous and likewise
Disconcerting—to be a thing, to be a thing
That *is*, that organizes other

Things into its own harmony
Or discord, sitting on a found sofa cluttered
With posies, contemplating The West

And her talking horses when out
Of the corner of your eye something rises against
The crisp blue winter sky

And you assimilate it, allow it
To manufacture in the peripheral
Coloring that inquires

Eye to word to ear—bluebird, bluebell
Bellbottom, and so
On, unraveling, a sea of cyborgs

Proliferating endlessly only
To end up jump
Cutting as one man lusts

After a curve and there are advertisers
Clamoring after its import, objects looming
Into our very *selves*, but this

Is no news to you, you
Live here every day, there are fish
Swimming and your hands

Have touched them, impossible
Notions have come to you as simply
As breathing, you don't fear

Your own sun, that which
Nurtures and browns
You, or you *do*, it terrifies you

Every morning, so it is with our minds
They make us these things
That are, and as such we stand

Apart from them, ladders interrogating
Half-curtained windows, I have
A trophy from coaching a girls' basketball

Team and it pleases me, the Atlantic
Is somewhere relatively close and I think
Of it rarely, as I did

The mountains of my youth, so you
Can tell I am no proprioceptivist
A fragile thing giddy at its own interior

Movements, the wet way a finger
Knows its duty among the twittering
Of its counterparts, I carry

On and if my mind wanders
Around the apartment
My body does not transiently

Abide, it directs, and so I affirm
The radio waves, Otis
Redding, even the stupidity

Of traffic, give me a pane to spy
Through and I will reflect
The world in its dubious elocution

Of forms, I don't have time
To rub my own eyes or
I have forever, a natural disaster

Strikes and all the animals survive, can't you
See what I'm saying, nobody is going
To give you permission, planets will go unnamed

Women will bathe, unprofitable
Beings will suffer terribly and smile
All the same, if god has to

Die so does jazz, all I'm asking
Is for a comely child to wrap
Its hand around one of my fingers

At the end—it will know what to do.

Misdiagnosis, or Funny Music next to Death

I wake to the sound of garbage
Trucks, hernia
Throbbing, my dream

Of an ex-girlfriend pixilated
Into the synaptic void, let me
Attempt to say this

Plainly—I am afraid
Of becoming a sad pervert, even
So I yearn for a life of direct

And unfettered humanity, suddenly today
It is the future and the sun
Is a laser beam dispassionately shooting

You in the eye, you
Being I, here, the uncalloused
Observer of daily, nay

Momently phenomena, such
As these children sledding the crusty
Hill on their little flotilla

Of screams, also the men erecting
Christo and Jeanne-Claude's *Gates*, one of them
Ravenously downing a hot

Sausage as the other
Will soon be absorbing all
Manner of foreign

Tourist only to spit them
Out at Columbus Circle to shop and be
Glum and so it is that I weary

At the confines
Of bitterness, the way
Things choke

On their own sustenance, how even glee
Is shot through with tiny darts
Of embarrassment, so unlike these

Fat, horny pigeons gurgling
Without cease, not that I'm proposing
That as an estimable kind of life, I

Who only yesterday thought
I was suffering
From a concussion and limped through

Grogginess and nausea, the two
Cloudbanking an acute
Terror of invisible bleeding before my fever

Broke thrice in the night and now
Things are looking up, the weather
Has reverted to climes

Less cruel, I'm losing
My attention for anguish, gnosis
Seems on parade as graffitied

Sunlight lingers on a barge of wet coal
And the nurse sleeps
In her terrific green pants

There's even a girl in the window
Teaching herself sign language
And laughing unself-consciously

Her hands fluttering
Like pennants in the wind, I know
These pleasures shadow

A deeper despair, but what
Good will come from
The mention of it? How our sour

Progeny have taken to
The indecent thoroughfares
Of youth, the way

You are channeling the orbit
Of a distant, inconsolable
Satellite, that I remain here, as always

Keeping the wolves from the door.

The True Meaning of Pictures

I never trusted in my ability
To wish for fear
Of misapprehending the implications

Of my desires, much
Less the desires
Themselves, like the sheer

Absurdity of trying
To hit a certain cloud
With a white

Balloon, all the while crossing
Your fingers that the winds will hold
It in shape, I do

Hope the rain will stay
Aloft until I reach the zoo
Today, I am curious

What kind of lonely
Creatures they've got locked
Up there, though lonely

Is better than dead, as I can tell you
From a trip I took stoned
To the San Francisco Zoo years

Ago, where my company momentarily lost
Our Frisbee in the giraffe pen
And Colin mustered all the heroic

Stupidity necessary to retrieve it, a little
Index card gracing each cage
With laments for the newly dead

Enumerated by their demeaning stage
Names: Bongo, Quiggly, etc.
And the lone remaining orangutan

Watched us with such
Anthropomorphic scorn, turning
His back, donning his chiffon

Robe and slowly walking away and since
Then I have felt that way
Many times, wondering just who

This spectacle actually
Entertains, each
Of us interminably caught

Moonlighting as both
Actor and director in a film
About the fantastic terror

Of existence, a comedy
Of course, and you get so fucking lost
In the production that it's days

Later, piss possibly running down your leg
That you remember to call cut, any wherewithal
Rubbing its red-streaked eyes

Somewhere in the back
Of your neck, so the question
Remains as to who exactly

Is shouldering the camera? You? The poem? I
Have seen pictures, only
Yesterday I watched a man's Bradburian

Tattoos leap from his torso and fly
Around the woods in search
Of a small girl while a woman

In the row before mine raked
At the air as if it were 1895 and we
Were caught in the path

Of a silent train, as if the earth
Were truly hurtling through
A widening sea of air we cannot breathe

I see pictures every day and by
God there is as much
Truth in them as in any shifting

Collection of thoughts, the lights
Abscond, cherries fill in, everywhere I go
People point out my wounds

And I can't contemplate the fact
Of having traipsed
The city these few weeks

Past with a gaping hole
In my leg, it's abominable
The way we let

Our feelings instruct
Us and yet
It's the only thing

To be done, right? Right?

American Music

I don't plan to address the physical
Impossibility of understanding
Death, but when you close my fingers

In your own, each bone comes
Alive, the skeleton jangles
In its perfunctory sleeve and even

As the bald man at the table
Next to ours thumbs
Through a magazine about guns

I can look out the window to where
A blossom of birds issues
From an abandoned skyscraper or traffic

Enacts its unwitting algorithms
Of pulse, it is in
This pulse that such thought

Arrives, in pulse
That it recedes, just as these city
Bodies orbit relative

To the attention they are
Paid, one eye
Ogling another, space

A capacity for the patent
Enumeration of our feelings
Some of them

Essential: love, carousal, wonder
Loss, breakfast, noise, terror, I refuse
The counsel of stupidity

Regarding such matters—this equals
That, take it from us, buy
A car, make loads of money only

To further the inventions
Of self, and so the dissociations
Of velocity continue unabated

Halving and trebling
Ourselves into metropolitan collage
Involved or unloved, the chalky

Abstinence or slick slip of our
Nowadays fraught
With a stubbornness to dissolve

Into pixels, our greatest
Poets hounded by lavender, the yelp
Of an old catamount plaguing

The suburbs, in Bhutan
It's said the local yeti survives
On a diet of frogs and I tend

To these stories carefully, knowing
The ease with which
An overly pleased public scoffs

At unsanctified dreams, my beard
Hedging outward as
Rote continuance happens

Only in the face
Of encapsulated truths, my truths
Equal suddenly to any

Small observation of cheer
The weeds reaching
Dutifully toward what gravity

Deems us opposite to, the sopor
Of a steadily impinging commonplace
And for the same reason

Each monarch is doomed
To revisit the same tree with the same
Poison, we think to

Lay our androgynous howling before
Suns of uninhabitable
Chemistry or *the lonely wail*

Of that old Cannonball blazing
Through the night, it's American
Music I have come to

Bring you you redoubtable ear.

The Detour of Everything That Happens

Landed in Albuquerque, drove
To Santa Fe, doves
Scattering in the driveway, my sister

Was reading about Mormons, my mother
About mystery in the Virgin
Islands, I slept under cowgirls on

Stale air and chased it
Each morning with too much
Coffee, a storm

Hit and the piñons dutifully
Bowed, a skunk rooted
Beneath the hot tub, near the night

Spider whose body resembled
A bird's egg and was plainly bejeweled
By a solitary diamond, all

Week I chucked rocks against the monotonous
Adobe, my shoulders turning
Pink, the clouds turning charcoal as so

Often ethics dwell in the driving
Out of fear, so that what
The centrifuge flings cannot

Malinger, so that
The fingers cannot remain
A flag draped idiotically

Across the eyes, *we need not be*
Let alone, we seek the acknowledgments
Of company amid

This cycling of refuted systems, the shocking
Green eyes of a young girl called
Kori widen as she tells me of elevators

The size of living
Rooms and I watch hummingbirds
Spar in abrupt fits over

A dish of sugar water as the late
Summer breeze makes
My forearm hair feel particularly

Inarticulate, receiving so much deciphering
So little as too often I invigorate
A line of discourse only to have it

Stump when the telephone
Rings, I dreamt I was a comedian
And the audience was

Laughing so hard I never
Was able to tell
A single joke, so here

It is—the work that I do does
Nothing to things, I leave home to imbibe
The dislocations of astonishment, to lose

My way and find another, tricking
The moments into line
Before defecting into rearrangements

And if I write to harbor
Squatters I am apart, these tremulous
Matters manic as

Each experience happens twice, even
The panic you feel returning
Home to a strange figure in the dark, even

If it turns
Out to be the innocuous
Shadow of a Buddha

Planted among the flowers in the garden.

Fertility for Dummies

Reads the book thankfully
Unread on the shelf, the glass
Gym across the park

Deserted, the tips
Of three of
My fingers have grown

Waxy, taut, things
Welling between the surface
And the bone as a lady

In an eggshell
Shawl pours over her
Copy of *Southern*

Accents only to lift
Her eyes from the page, lean
Across the table and leer

At me, increasing my ever-present
Paranoia that strangers
Can read the intimate portraits

I make of them and will any
Minute be thrusting
A sharp part of their body

Against mine and now snow
Has begun to flutter
And circle tentatively beyond

The panes like some Felliniesque
Spring wildly jumping
The gun, this Thursday

Languor could use such an Italian
Commotion, the impromptu
Bonfire flush against a sudden and cartoonish

Bosom, it is in
This way that my biology attends
To the shapes my looking

Constructs and I am here
To appreciate the manner in which
A smoking woman

Wades through asphalt, how
One building dwarfs
A larger one merely by the affect

Of its character, the way the boy
Impatiently cultivates
His inviolate sheen, combing

The grates with his eyes, his fists
Hidden but surely
Balled, not often am I

Prepared for violence, though I find it
Natural, in me as in
The world, and it remains

Revolting, *the brief*
Desire to trample something
Living, loving certain

Registers of collapse, tiny pockets
Bereft of grief, it reminds me how Henry
Miller spent three years

Inside a slide
Trombone and I have
Found myself too

Sane, and sullen, and suddenly
I feel just like Bonnie
Raitt on the cover of *Streetlights*

Her mouth unself-consciously
Open, a little
Question in her

Eyes as if
To say, "I am so
Full of this...

This... what *is* this?"

Horoscopic Brushstrokes in the Margin of Death

Ever noticed how a flame disappears
In sunlight, even while
Notorious lightning breeds

On the horizon, you
Have an eye
For such things—the reactivation

Of long-malingered volcanoes, the manner
In which a wounded sloth
Creeps lamely from unwieldy trunk

To bending branch, the plaintive
Varieties of unseen matter
Coalescing against our lamentable screen

Of den culture, you are the kind
Of person who puts things in order in
Order that the edgeless

Fog might disband, if only
For an afternoon, and this is why we have
Come to you, repeatedly swearing

That we're not animals, that
The fact is we would not dream of having them
Sullied by our petty transactions of faith

And discord, we want you
To think about us
Like an eye that has been turned

Hopelessly inward
So all it sees is a miasma
Of tissue, tiny parts

Convulsing involuntarily, absurdly
Divorced from their original functions, one
Cannot love that way, just as

One cannot enter the fold with his nails
Thrashing the air he cannot
Breathe, you *know* this, your very

Gestures have instructed
Us thus, the way they disassemble the easy
Grotesque we have become and point

Toward a prospect of grace, only last
Night you made apologizing
Pretty again, perhaps this evening

The dogs will lay supplicant
At our feet and think us masters
When for so

Long it's been the reverse, tomorrow untold
Colonnades of light might
Descend from the weightless vault

Of heaven, because, you see, that's a possibility
As all things suddenly
Are, one has only to speak

Your name and a massive flock of dirigibles
Arranges itself into graph
Paper patterns against the amoebic

Sky, I
Would only ask that you take off
Your jacket and sit here

In the chair beside my bed, I must
Shortly leave this only-just-this-very-instant
Brightening world, and I would

Have your perfect
Hand laid heavy atop
The loosening

Furrows of my bead-covered brow.

I Am Not a Cinematographer

Winter has grown
Late, intrepid
Profiles momently

Gracing the construction
Barrier with weightless charm, a nearly
Chinless woman flashes me

Her smile only to withdraw it, seeing
That I too am headed
West, I feel as if I stare at women

All day long, a by-product of my being
Alone all night, so down
24th Street I go, casually flitting

From gallery to gallery, Cecily Brown
Surprisingly mute while farther
Along I am greeted with a pleasantly ribald

Exhibition of buxom lady pirates, all
The while anticipating the purloined sandwich
In my bag, a thing

That pleases
Me greatly, as does the birthmark
On the bridge of the nose

Of the girl in the deli
Buying a Diet Pepsi, like I said
I don't want to die

A sad pervert, but I'm not yet ready
To apologize for this undirected
Throbbing and the desire for a life of direct

Coincidence, my annoyance
Growing at the protracted twitter
Of teenagers squeezing

Their way to Madison to shop
And make phone calls and soon I am
Mired in each

Intricacy of space, knee
To hand, eye taking in a mouth
As it talks almost

Disembodied, a woman's narrow
Currinesque nose bifurcating the slope
Of her chest and of course

You do not make sense
Of it, you make conversation, even alone
These little interjections

Of desire tipple at the eyes' wet
Scan, which is not to say I am like an actor
Who ends up resembling

The characters he's played, I am
Not even a cinematographer wrenching
Beauty from an otherwise

Dumb panorama, I *am* that dumb
Panorama, the trees, windows
The very avenues themselves and you

Are the camera, both of us
Caught in the dizzying, phenomenal
Exchange as it

Zooms like an electron
Between our shells, bouncing
Jaggedly, so that

One might run
One's mouth forever, lips
Flapping like a moth

Full of blood and never quite pin
It down, our wants so
Jubilantly bent on parallax

Our wishes always scurrying
Vague for fear of being
Irreversibly misconstrued

By a capricious god, the fact
That you could get everything you ever
Wanted and then find that you

Aren't *that* you anymore and still
We insist on this death
We die not dying, all that's left

Is to find something impossible
And spend your entire life
Invisibly nearing it, we are constantly on

Trial, our bodies break, our needs
Consume us, I see
A darkness and I can't believe

How strange it is to be anything at all.

The Asymptotic Approaches

I woke to the laughter of a friend from
A dream of life
Caught in the balance

Between teleology
And the moment, finding spires
To be merely sideways

Horizons and the sky
An infinite instant
Carelessly looming supine

Above our heads, this is why *sexuality*
Is not a reflex, the intentions
Of a cloud wait patiently to be

Coupled to the eye, which in
Touching the newspaper relates to me
Partial things, my friend

Ben tends to shake
Superfluous things from the tips
Of his fingers, some car

Things like an immaculate
Animal at the far
End of 16th Street, for

My ear has its own crass
Manner of making phantoms
Of beauty into

Familiar symbols, I say the earth
Is not unfriendly, the end is not always
Deadly, when the desert

Closes one in
Its alien
Throat and discloses

Its whispery valence the sun
Leaves his perfect
Shadows strewn like capes

Upon the dazzling
Promiscuities of America, picture
That on the side of a bus

Bisecting Park Avenue as a song
Sings *men make sense*
When they prevail, I make

The bed, turn on
The light over the turtle's
Head and catch the 6

Uptown, tonight I will register
The pornographic
Constellating of smog-woozy

Stars, but here the man
Daydreams with his fading tattoos
Peeking from beneath white

Sleeves and a previous
Occupant has left a crossword
For me to complete, pen

Jabbing my thigh, my thought
Distracted by its *asymptotic*
Approach to reality, we are never

Quiet, never quite
Free from the hallucinations
Of meaning, the feather

In the hat of the woman is not even
The limit of her
Body and as it stirs within

The passersby, I say to myself *I*
Have made your body
Hurt, the weather says *hope*

I get the wind right
This time, Hiroyuki Doi says *suppose*
Every creature is a circle that exists

In this world, how many of them can I draw?

There Will Be a Very Meaningful Picture Here

In the recurring caveman
Dream I wear my meat vest
And I love you, the whites

Of our eyes gleaming
Like cleanly picked bones as we sit
Beside our fire, the one that

Allows us to think
Outside predation and weather
And I wonder

If I would have the time
To love you otherwise, a thought that
Unsteadies me horribly, like

Yesterday, in the hands
Of the pear-shaped Russian
Hairdresser, the way

She sylphlike peered
At me in the silent glass
Of the mirror, her

Clicking scissors slipping
Behind my ear and I wanted
To sleep in her terrible

Black pupils, this is what haircuts
Mean to me, I am as a beast
Dressed in the guise of a boy, I wish

For a small, ardent thing
And am throttled by
The lung-crushing collapse

Of my own desire as it comes
Into being, which is
Why I prefer the hallucinations

Of Neanderthal life, days
Spent inching
Boulders from the ridge

Where below a pitching pack
Of mastodons tread trumpeting and nights
Where my dream

Within my dream is of riding
The mountainous
Eremotherium, a creature

Whose yawning bellow fills
Forests where birds once ruled
The earth, but we, luckily

Have no such ambition, plastic
Bags drift in the bare
Arms of the trees we know

Not the names of, a sunlit
Satellite dish dithers
Next to a still, iron weather vane

And we sleep in an old bed, our fire
Crumbling down to embers, your hand
Probing for morsels in my stiff

Knotted hair, I remove
My meat vest and I love
You, our bulbous

Noses flickering in the ash-flecked night.

Rhinoceros

I was born in the middle
Of the end of
A decade in the middle

Of the end of
A century, my fingers
Always slightly

Shaking, holding them
Out to the various people I am
Thinking to love

The people who sit me
Down, explain
How very inside of it

I am, charging, a thought
Bubble blotted
Woodpecker red, the come

Down of our terrifying
Anatomies as four
Hands thoughtlessly clutch

At the flash an airplane
Casts across the lawn, sky
Cloudless, noise

Sudden as every twelve minutes
Or so the shadow
Solemnly passes, a squabble

Of birds igniting among
The flickered blades of the lawn
This is how language

Malingers harmless things, each being busy
Dreaming in their sliced self
Self-portrait skin, the painting reads

PAY FOR SOUP, BUILD
A FORT, SET THAT ON FIRE
The song sings *most*

Of my fantasies are of making someone else
Come as the young transient
Sweats sleeping beneath the unbudded arms

Of the cherry tree on the esplanade
Where I too lay, my head on
The stomach of a dark-haired girl

Who says I've been coagulating
My whole life it seems
Only to dissolve, *to speed*

Sleep, dream, and thaw.

Horse Stories

The sun is a headache
I take with me from place
To place, a duck's

Yammering green skull
Beaded with lake, I wonder
Who turned on

All the birds today? A young Slovenian
Woman reads Kant between bites
Of ice-cream sandwich as the kindergarten

Children impersonate a chain
Gang staggering astride
Their flimsy string, no one is sleeping

In the thicket for once, no
Suffering lady stuck
Interrogating the strangeness

Of air, though a man in pinstripes
Is resolutely wading circles
Into the cluttered water of the fountain

His expensive leather shoes
Shuffling among the hopefully
Abandoned coins, so it

Is to myself I
Must trust the bearings of this
Massless core, the good

With which it binds
Me to the world and would
That we were possessed

Of even more
Meddlesome middle, sentries
Of self to crowd out

The frightened relativity
Of postmillennial
Behavior, I have or

I hate, a soul is not
A gauge, no
Thing receding, expanding

So it is if
I crush two mine
Does not treble

Nor divide into thirds as the ice
Cream has now melted down
The stick onto her fingers, pasting

The book's pages, my knees
Thoughtlessly knocking, a pigeon
Narrowly missing the ear

Of a small girl as her mother
Screams in terror, everybody turning
Terrified and when

Later the man on
The subway train states
My name is

Sonny Pain I know
Exactly what he
Means, names being our

Small, initial admissions of guilt.

Hockey Night

Flank half in
Shadow, bulging palomino
Terrified by a rich

Lady's dog, it's true we all
Stagger in the face
Of contraries, as in the stead

Of truth we find evidences
Not forthcoming, you
Carry a little set of demons through

The world between its words
And what remains
Unsaid, bubbles of thought

Swaying obscure
In the dusky skyscraper light
Of 3 p.m., 23rd Street

The fifth day of the fifth
Month of the fifth
Year since the disillusionment

Of the millennium, I stop
Into the Andrea
Rosen Gallery, snag

A handful of Felix
Gonzalez-Torres coffee
Candies, turn

Flush into the monolith
Denouement, its feedback
Score airily haunting

The alleyway with sparkles
Of porous fuzz, next
Thing I know I'm in San Francisco

Treading fog, a 40 oz. bottle
Wrapped in the shopkeeper's daughter's
Homework, a moment

Then St. Paul, the Mississippi
Gurgling slackly beneath the cars
Of commuters fleeing

To the suburbs as our ghost
Town recommences and someone left
A crate of apples

In the parking lot, but despite
Our best efforts to eat
Them they begin to rot, so Sunday

We hungover haul
It to the tracks and as a train
Passes we deliriously

Fling as many as we can, each skin
Ripping almost before it
Leaves our hands, mine again thrust into slowly

Dissolving pockets, skeleton
Night pervading, the fume-ridden periphery
Of Union Square abuzz

With transient glee, fiery rituals
Of carousal recapitulating
Before my eavesdropping eyes, my friends

You are never far
From mind, from ear, from there
To here we continue

To thrash and smoke, we flare
Through winter atop
Our wiry bones, we barrel

Headlong and *we are the ones.*

Surviving Desire

Erupting from
The Carroll Street tunnel the graffiti
Reads CHOKES

HIS CHICKEN EVERY NIGHT and we
The wan passengers
Convene momentarily, our anonymous lot

Suspended slant, about
To nosedive on the dingy everyday
Landscape of traffic

And ruin, rivet-studded
Girders grumpily trellising
The smog-blue-gray

Sky, May and too
Many mornings have I spent
This week observing

The recumbent figures
Of capital tragedy
Their scaly ankles dangling

From soot-soured Wranglers, likeness
Likewise suspended in favor
Of a proximity, our teetering off

And on pattern of tapering
Parabola shapes arbitrarily weaving
Depths and it depends

On the curious phases a face
Makes wincing at nature, the maturing
Content of cells, can you see this

Sound collecting there in spastic
Syllable growths? It's cyclical
The way one devours his own carefully

Tended ignorance, a slow
Canceling of accumulated skew
As the mutilations fall

Off and are just as quickly
Replaced by others, the spell
One conveniently

Forgets, the mask one
Tries on and unobservantly
Absorbs, the train's

Sibilant burble hurrying
Forth as the signal greens and I
See nothing

Barely beneath this
Concrete, no lurid node
Pulsing beyond

The sky's stately
Dome, who demands this forever
Grope after the mysteries

Of a sphere eaten by worms
Regurgitated by birds
Paralyzed by windowpanes? We are all

Forced to mourn at the outrageous
Tombstones these towers make, rifling 100 percent
Cotton clouds as a little girl

In a purple sweater chases a brown
Pigeon along the platform's orange edge, believing
Is a form of expectation, *tonight*

I shall dream of newspapers
Wrapped in fish, of smog wrapped
In skin as sometimes

I tremor at the way
The world seems so vigorous
One second and the next

It's swimming, each dumb leaf
Resorting to metaphor
As every winking turn traps

You into thinking that life
Is a meticulous plot dimly allotted
To you alone, people

Topple, transubstantiation
Fails, we fall into knowing before
We know that

Knowing is not enough.

Recommence Everything

If I am to be committed
To transcendence, *to merely say that*
There is a body is not

Yet to deal with it, if my looks go
Everywhere they are
Selfsame slaughtered by the manner

In which they snag, a car
Illuminates in panic every thirteen
Minutes or so and it's driving

The neighbors nuts, as the socioeconomic
History of golf pollutes
The branch in the hand of the kid

Swinging at an imaginary
Ball, handshakes
Here are reversible, we touch

Touching the way these fall dragonflies
Flee the invisible weft
They sew into the air uniting

Above our heads, today's weather
Report calls for abundant
Sunshine as a man with a limp

Plods past the girl
Asleep in her tiny camouflage
Bikini and if she dreams

Of *the secret blackness*
Of milk, it's only these pinks
Lazily invading

A sigh descending
Over the scene as all the girls
Put on their shirts and we

Must recommence everything
Just moments
After it's begun, the sun

Shining abundantly
Down upon the clouds, or briefly
Breaking on the totality

Of a dog, our eyes bent
On tracing the invisible, there's something
About lived life that leaves

Itself in intractable
Tufts upon the heart, it's tough
Being a thing

That understands enough
Of what it means to be
Seen to see others in the nightmare

Of consciousness, which is nonetheless
A dream, which is finally
Choice without choice, spiraling

Like the intertwined black
And white on the disk
Of the hypnotist, whose colors

Remain fixed, we remain
Unconvinced by the spectacular
Passing of modes, want

Our ears near the frequencies
Of *I hear myself*
With my throat and *what the throat*

Thinks we drink, let
Each cell in your body bulge
With song, there is room

Enough for more: a mouth, a moon, again.

The Science Fiction of Color

At Delancey a man
Babbles with his neck
On his chest

Like a bib, a teenage girl allows
Her leg to dangle over
A startled teenage boy, both laughing

Their window in the twenty-second
Commercial of childhood, our attention
Wavering as the world

Does, petals
Of neglect shedding
At the periphery

Of the eye, knowledge subsumed
By our desire for desire, only
Today I discovered John McEnroe

Owns Gerhard Richter's *Girl*
On a Donkey, the nature of perversion
Perpetually shifting as one's dream

Dwindles in the lens
Or is lost adrift
The swifts' delirious plunge

As gentle earthquakes pervade
As the little tear gland
Says *tic-tac* and petty octogenarians

Crowd the Lexington
Storefronts where white girls
Spill their blank

Guts between pages in the cloud
Book, waiting for Max
Ernst's Science Fiction of Color

Summer correspondence
Course to begin, each
Benign conscience quietly plagued

By the interregnum, it is not trivial
This death we die not
Dying, the blur of sexuality

Metastasizing in blinks, I never
Imagined I'd marry
An aristocrat, nor quote

The adages of some thickly accented
Bavarian, *some stupidity*
Is heroic, some heroes assume

The village children
Are blind, I can't
Count the number of times

I've thought the world
Different only to find my fingers
Twittering in their familiar

Way, the reflective scallops
My nails make shaking
Like gusts furrowing a sail

And so I too am too
Fraught with this calligraphic
Landscape we speed

Too sure these unsteady words
Are like a frowning woman who wants
Desperately not to sleep

Here tonight, if reality
Is temporal why not write
Poems the size

Of cathedrals, at Fourth Avenue
The conductor howls, the dreaded
Man sings *Ain't no*

Sunshine as the sunshine
Streams through keyed plastic, a mother
Gabs on her phone as her baby

Bellows and that's life
In the ten-second
Opening of train doors don't

Be afraid to give everything away.

Grandpa Was a Salesman

It's the day the day
Everyone else is vacationing
At Fire Island, the gleam

In the glasses of the *Business Man Business
Man* peddling Duracell AAs
From car to car, coloring the inevitable

Thrill I feel being
Surrounded by insolent creatures
Daring someone to fuck

With them on their commute, while the dreary
Sonic lassitude of burned-out
Churches skewers the horizon or a wall

Map gone secretly
Glue under *the cramped corpse-light
Blue of an airplane bathroom*

The sign of the defunct
Psychic persists, a distant foal
Stammers, stamps, and who

Is responsible for crowding the world
With such a cowardly delirium
Of thoughts, the soft focus of death

Rifling each tacky eye
Of the passersby, all of us mired
In the pithy forensics these

Contagious dreams
Gravitate toward, I like
To get stupid

With my friends, to get nostalgic
In the dusky resettlement
Of chances, Ben wrote a poem

When he was seven
About a robot made entirely
Of panthers, yesterday I

Squeezed my bicycle past
A sleeping man meticulously
Wrapped in Mylar

And this has become a study
For a larger ancestral
Portrait, this poem was actually

Purchased in Beijing in 1890
For a handful of silver
Fillings, I was doomed to sneeze

Constantly until my braces
Were removed, my dad
Used his own pliers, a practical

Response to lack, you see, Grandpa
Was a salesman who drank
Half a dozen Coca-Colas every

Afternoon, his mother had twenty-two
Children, three sets
Of twins, all of whom died, as did

She, before she was fifty, before
I was born and it strikes me
That every person in every passenger

Seat in every car in
Every town in every country
Is selling some goddamn

Thought to themselves, but you see
Grandpa was a salesman, both
Of them, that's why I have my foot in this

Door and my knuckles are red and I'm smiling.

ZieherSmith Dispatches

The backward fire seeps
Into its blooming
Woodpile as the poet mispronounces

Masturbatory, pinwheels
Of elk lining
The otherwise white

Walls wink, their fractal
Patterns coalescing
With the languid frenzy of

Birds aligning the unassigned
Capacities of the city
And tonight I am a cormorant

Whose neck expands
At will, my heart
Too loud and these lyrics kill

The saturation we
Become tracing
Ourselves into air, a jay

Crowds a turtledove
From the clothesline nobody
Uses, scatology trumps

Tenderness, the ovoid frames
Of a girl's glasses
Clash with the rectangle

Face she was born
Within and what of
The part of

Me that embraces
What I loathe or how
A glove pierces

Its useless quotient
Of rain, the only meaningless
Catastrophe is the one

So large everybody can suck
It away in pieces, each
Minor fiasco gradually engulfed

By the vacuum it generates, if I was
Writing the blurb for this
Decade it would read *miraculous*

In its quack solemnity, I am going
Tubin' this weekend and that
Propels me, you see I like to get stupid

With my friends, to court the favor
Of gales, to stare feline
As the variously colored entrance

Tickets to the Brooklyn Museum spin
On the blades of my ceiling
Fan or to sit enthralled at the mouth

Of the Union Square subway
Noting how our corporeal
Parentheses are so fantastically

Split, the song
Says *it ain't natural for you to cry*
In the midnight, but I

See the guitar soundless
In its gently imperceptive hum
The way the dew

Removes itself and the poet
Has not yet understood
The consequence of friendship

She asks if she should go on.

Blood on the Tarmac

In Brooklyn I contemplate
What curious maladies are borne
By the surprise drip

Of sixth-floor air
Conditioners effusively
Placating heat

But here, static, out
The window of seat 6A
I see blood

On the tarmac, its elegant
Maroon arch like
One half of a pelvis

And as the voice pervades
Enumerating our emergency
Procedures, I make it

A point to visualize
Grand catastrophes in the hope
Of deflating

The cruel whimsy
Of a capricious god, in the back
A young child

Vaults its merciless
Incomprehensibility from the shallow
Of its toothless mouth as we

Begin to roll and soon
We're aloft, the cemetery
A muted computer

Chip and the impossible
Sky like itself only
Vaster, bluer, two and a half

Hours later once
Again piercing the shaggy
Moguls of cloudtop

To reveal green protractor
Ballfields and myriad
Swimming pools unblinking

Along the dumb, patchwork face
Of the suburbs, I turn
Off my electronic device

Thinking there is
No jet engine where there
Is no mind

There is no love in
The unerring, no embrace
Where the wind is

Absent and what
Is it to explode
But the pencil-point

Extension of learning?
To evolve except
A heightened susceptibility

To the brutal modicums
Of furthering control? Thousands
Of glimmering autos

Wait in their anonymous lots
As we fall upon
Minnesota, the last

Place I could be called
Innocent and since then
My ignorance has

Not stopped alarming
Me, not grown
Less than a compounded sum

Of my experience so
There is no love in the one
True path just

As there is a canceling sweetness
In the poem's last
Line, awkward thunder

In the airplane's furious deceleration
And warm distance in each
Of the loved ones you return

To from so very far away.

For

Another March arrives
You wake to the hydraulics
Of the 75 bus

As a man you have scarcely
Met dies and you lose
Another indispensable compass

The fluorescent wanderings
Of your eye divorced
From the tolerant measure of his and we

Can't escape the luggage language
Makes of our thought, detours backwardly
Spelling out whatever finds

Itself wrung from moment's lurch, my friends
There is no reasonableness
Fit, no gray grand arbiter of sense

To fix the tangle, no way
Of knowing what and whom we need
Most alive, as today

My love's eyes are like little
Animals opening
And closing in order

That I might survive, I feel
To live in them as a page
Must, I wake and want nothing

Of the lonesomeness of being
Closed and connected
Only by the taut physicality

Of spines, to shore again against
The smallness of the real, the horror
Of living forever

Interred within a reasonable universe
Because there is no
Impenetrable line, the months

Pass, dust gathers, a cut
On the bridge of the nose vanishes
And meaning slips in

And out of view, like stars
Surfacing on a night
Sky scalloped by cloud

Cover, your love's shapely
Thighs tremble and detonate
An irresolution

That's been terrifying
To bear intangibly for the past
Year or so, here

Are a few of the reasons
To continue: *For Love*, for *The Immoral
Proposition*, for *All*

That Is Lovely in Men.

Consequent Realities

My love is studying
Anatomy and I
Am a dilettante resuscitating

The moaning anomie
Of postmillennial drudgework
Into daily veer

As Watts teenagers writhe
And jolt like the victims of electricity
We diminish them

To be, an earnest rage born
Of the absurd, a fit
Response to an irresponsible

Age, each morning's paper
Soaked in a bloom
Of limbs, each ironing

Wretch wrought by the incidentals
Of a life unwittingly
Defended by a spectacle

Of death, I myself often
Pass this
Way with my hands

Over my eyes, hopelessly
Mired by the gross
Mitigation of routine

As the recursion of the
Spreadsheet self
Grows misty, harmonies

Invade, the *Voyager*
Ages in direct
Proportion to my own ungainly

Orbit and literature wreaks
Its unstoppable
Pageant of obituaries

On the American lunch
Break, my great
Grandfather was adopted

At the Battle of Wounded Knee
And I called him Bernie
And I swear we will not be confined

To *pale little moments*
Of exuberance or the inexhaustible
Shifting of these consequent

Realities, it is impossible
To measure how
Often the phantom

Limbs of memory return bent
On self-mutilation, nails
That aren't there firmly dug

Into a palm that no
Longer exists, though it
Does, has, always

Will it seems, aligned
With the body's bewildering
Pulse, the eye's fiery

Recapitulation of difference
And who will stand
With us against the relativism

Of sensory input? When
Is it but constantly
That these assumptions threaten

To overtake us? Who deigns
To bring my love
And me something to wear we feel

Like getting out of bed.

Independence Day

I was trying to land
A plane in the Andes only
To wake to

The squealing brakes of garbage
Trucks once again, the soft
Focus of death reflected in a pigeon's

Rooftop warble, this is
What it means
For me to be in love

To swallow grief
In wondrous subvocal
Gulps, I think

Of all the fingers
Wriggling in their crepuscular
Pocketlight and wish

The cloistered sublimities
Of touch to open
When the singer says *feeling*

He says it seven
Times and the rain that wasn't
Due until evening falls

In tiny drops against
The ketchup of your hotdog
Everyone in preparations

To watch America
Swim, Long Beach lifeguards
Drowned out by the shrill

Calamity of spangled
July, this is a film
About the ankles of a man

Cornered in the alleyway
By a sudden vortex
Of refuse, a song about a woman

Trembling in relief
At the absence
Of life, her windshield

Speckled with elliptical
Distortions, the day
Calamitous and it was I who

Dubbed the cat *Thirsty* and I
Who staked claim
To *Dirt Bottle Island*

Where spokes of illumination came
Crashing through its canopy
To fill the meticulous scatter of glass

With glints, your shins
Ornamented by scars, one
Hand around my

Waist, the other flat
Against your lips and you
Have said nothing

Of me until you reckon
With my unreasonable yen
For Midwestern meat

Salads and the weekly catharsis
Of montage, I
Who left Colorado

To revel in the obscene
Pageant of tender idiots we call
Art, to fail in

Habituating the scotomas
Of class, to daintily
Hone these new hallucinations

Into viable texture
And listen as
The baby downstairs cries

Out to the world its astonishment.

I Ghost

If I say I
Am romantic, I mean that
Any beauty that persists

In abstraction does not belong
To me, any longing
That does not conspire

With me nose
To nose is inoperable and *little*
By little it came to me

That walking along the street I am
Saying something even
The streetlamps are doomed

To repeat, to
Embattle within, to illuminate
Without, I dictate

The illiterate ramblings
Of the F beneath the softball
Outfield, buy a new

Hula hoop at the carousel
Concession stand and envelop
The blood-coursing

Hands of a dark-haired girl under
The surveillance of many
Horses, lions, and giraffes lifting

And sinking in the paradox
Of frozen motion, if I
Say I ghost hummingbird-like

Among the braids
Bobbing atop a toddler's skull, I mean that
Nothing is safe

From these interventions
Of sense and *the color
Of the human face is not less*

Mysterious, I remember the broken
Nose of the man who taught
Me how to kill with the sound

Of my hands clapping as I emerge
Into the eerily natural
Light descending on Astor

Place, thinking again
About the quirks
Of anatomy, how they

Resurface, how even the disciples
Of disciples have disciples, returning
Danger to the tiny

Inner disturbances we share, your tongue paused
On my neck, your nails grazing
My back, I cautiously pray we *have the good*

*Fortune to avoid the habits
Of reduction* and I would have my ceiling suffocated
With aerial photographs of the Nebraska

Plain where my mother was
Taught to read, red
Rectangles abutting black, beige

And the occasional green, or Queens
Just before eleven o'clock
At night, its pulsing nebula

Congregating in veins the way
The body's discarded
Hair gathers in airy balls

Beside the radiator, the subway
Warns *if you see*
Something say something

And that's exactly what I intend to do.

The Harmony of Overwhelming

Perhaps I exist to ruin
Objectivity, to dull
The shears that this insular

Art becomes, our proclivities
Mingling in the mangling
Street, since I moved to New York

I have not stopped
Sneezing, though I did pause
In writing this poem

To hunt down a fearsome
Silverfish, which undulatingly flew
Across the keys, even

If it never sleeps
It does awaken and one peculiar
Moment you find yourself

In the unfriendly grip
Of the octopus so
Is it in vain that I hope

To be less of a stranger
To you while at the same time trying
To avoid the disgrace of being

Well known? The city is
Harmonious mass, an Amazon
Of commerce, even

If it is *the harmony of overwhelming*
And collective murder, I had expected to lose
My virginity to my babysitter

At the age of twelve, Breton
Wished to keep the book
Ajar, the song says *I can't be held*

Accountable for the things
That I've seen, but I refuse to
Deny the refuse

Of our lives the warmth
Of witness, I will not submit
Myself to loopholes

In recursion, the only phone
Call I got all
Day was a wrong

Number, yet that also
Has not stopped
Me from feeling a consequent

Note among many, kind
Words no less
Instructive and I'm off

To the zoo for distant salutations
To the wallaby I've dubbed
Bushwick Bill, also to look in

On a deteriorating letter
I've stuck between the wires
Of a fence running

Along the ravine, all my
Life I've dreamt
I was able to see translucent

Arrows composing the air and thought
It feasible to spend
An afternoon not breathing

But when I stop
To remind myself of the way you
Smell when we're lying

In bed I know it
Would be a terrible waste
Not unlike the beauty

Of insects, this apparitional
Night, this soft, silly
Music that has become more

Meaningful than I could imagine.

Flouting Determinism

We eat afternoon
To bones in
A metropolis where ghosts

Are always hungry, their vivisected
Steam-plume quotations
Coddled by racket or carved

Into disappearing paper
Snowflakes against the charcoal
Doors, all these

Memories pass in
The way veins
Collapse, little bruises

Surfacing on twice
Exposed film, I do not wish
To wash the fingerprints

From my thought nor burnish
An age made rough
By understanding, I imagine the cat

Dreams of a fluttering
Hand in a lush
Leafy darkness, when I was

Twelve there was nothing
More pleasant than the startling
Ping of crab

Apples hitting hoods and here
I am disheartened
By *the flat, arid music*

Of Western imperialism, its accord
Looming, the epiphanies
Gutted, but all parts are not

Pieces, if the eyes close most
Often to open
Upon the diminishing

Grandeur of amputated scenes
They ebb only
To bare the imperative

Quality contained therein and one has
But to walk the deserted
Halls of a museum to know

How much life these portraits
Need gathered about, how much trouble
Resides in the definite

Mind when *our best defense*
Against terrorist attacks is to be late
To work, my love

Loves me enormous and the coincidence
Of these emotions dispels
Dogma in the same way it spells

Out a burdensome absurdity, my sister
Fears the introduction
To her book will cast a wraithlike

Pall over the remainder but
I apprise her
Of certain things:

(1) all well-intentioned beginnings
(2) wander in the hope
(3) of flouting determinism

The wolfman weeps
Half-conscious in the unfinished
Suburban development

As here in the botanical gardens
The turtles stretch their necks for sun
And my god if the turtles

Are sticking their necks out why aren't we?

Neurological Theories of Denial

Heat seeps to sprinkle
My forehead with sweat just as every
Morning we return to the cold

Liberty of distance, droves
Of the enchanted exchanging
Lives, I will build

A strange child to reckon
With such horror and cause
It to seek absences

To stare at truth like a gleaming
Toxicity translated by
Breezes and it will glean

Also the private conspiracy
One makes with
Oneself, for *if we are*

One with explosion
It is combinatorial, the ice
Cream man's melodic

Transience merging with the human
Traffic as bodies perpetuate
Their chemical escapade, ardently reveling

In the catalog of soft
Abstractions, when you are gone I listen
To *The Transfiguration* and am lost

In the cloud your body
Becomes, I mean
The one you possess

That which possesses me
In the eerie stereo darkness
And if *grammar*

Is the direct result of how
Humans feel in the world, perhaps
The obverse is also

True, adverbs make me who
It is I can be said
To have been, I can practically

Hear all those words out
There amassing to make the journey
Inward, blistering

Pings and haunted *whooshes*
Triangulating at the self's all too
Permeable periphery

As if it were no
Surprise to suddenly dissolve
Into a tome-like tomb

Of syllabic feedback, the poems
That these days
Have become more

Real than the indentations
On my mattress or
An unwashed cutting

Board, this cigarette in the empty
Beer can atmospherically
Sizzling to its obscure close

On the streetside sill, so
It is that a man
Marvels at the tumult

Or ease he's
Become, balancing the neurological
Theories of denial

With the fact that the heart is still
Beautiful as a seismograph
That if I dare to stare a stranger

In the eye his palms
Will swell and that it is suicide to live
Conscientiously among

The compromising throng.

Subcutaneous Concerns

Ambling down the summer
Midnight streets of New York
One gets the distinct

Impression of drifting between the walls
Of a clammy cave, lamps
Like masses of bioluminescent

Fungi casting orange
Light into the grumbling depths
Of the subway

Grates, my friend
Quit his job at the greeting card
Factory in St. Paul, a woman

I know saw little animated
Tennis shoes every time she closed
Her eyes, I close

My hand around a fork
And eat saffron rice and black
Beans with jalapeño

Pickled carrots from a Tupperware bowl
While watching the horse
Breaking scene from *The Misfits*

That purportedly killed
Clark Gable, his stubborn heels
Dug into Nevada's

Desolate earth, it's so late
In the history of literature, so shot
Through with older raptures

That chime dustily
Upon the shrinking bell
Of The West, once

I drove 4,000 miles to realize all
My ideas were still in Ohio
All my kindhearted abominations fed

Into a tiny voltage
Of axons and yet nothing
Compares to the melt

I feel watching
NECKFACE's glory fritter
Away on the rooftops

Of the Gowanus Canal, this stunning
Industrial eyesore where I used
To walk hand in hand with a lady of German

Descent, I know a man
Who was mistaken
For a bear, a town where all

The hamburgers are
Named after chess moves, a chasm
In the elevated parking

Lot where we've buried three Christmas
Trees and tomorrow I shall flash
My thighs upon the river, shall wed

My friend to a keg but tonight
The subcutaneous
Concerns dawdle unmet

By the dizziness of glee, stray
Cats call out their lust
Or terror or both and the guitar

Can be heard just by looking at its strings.

Lo

My first wire
Job was a fortune
Of violets

And I dismantled them
To flee my own
Flaxen locks in a pot

Of coffee, it was my destiny
To spend the summer on the porch
Lifting a dumbbell

And now here
I am programming daffodils
In the guise of leisure

The girls of Windsor
Terrace propped against Sabella
Pizzeria's glass doors, I never

Made claims to portraiture
Am merely a sketch
Artist, a draftsman gracelessly

Devising devices to further
A kind of compassionate absurdity
Like the words in the bathroom

Of the Buttermilk
Bar, which read 20,000
LEAGUES UNDER

MY NUT SACK
But also like the Nobel Prize
Winning novelist who

Writes *Because I own this*
Rifle, my arms and legs
And blood and bones are superior to yours

For man treads perverse
Among the mute
Consciousnesses, he is a she

And we are all of us
Stunning in the magnetic
Fields we toil

Over, the saliva of our tongues flung
Before us as they dart
This way and that, panderers

To the throne of the Frog
King, who eyes us suspiciously
And *ribbits* with the full

Timbre of his royal blood
For he too has seen the girls
Outside the pizzeria

Their plaid knee-skirts
Stained with yellow garlic knot
Grease, he guesses

At the rude waves
Of heat which sluggishly billow
From an idle downtown

Bus and he fears the bodega
Cat napping near a bag
Of quarter-chips as the palpitations

Continue, we dwell in a constant
State of self-immolating
Gasps and yet there is something elegant

In it, the way we glance
The commiserations
Of biology and the abstract sexuality

Of time contours bleaker
Existences, there are so many
Pregnant women in July

And I would ask you to wait
With me here, watch the incandescence
Of bodies abut

On these gum-covered walks, if only
To catch one or two
As they verily pass through

The ever-humiliating impasse of desire.

An Introduction to the Mechanics of Deformable Bodies

When Erica says
I am feeling myself and jovial
I think of the orange

Tipped trees between
The buildings out
My window, their penknife

Leaves grazing like air-bound anemones
Haunted by the jellyfish
Forms of black plastic bags, today

You turn yet another
Year older, youth
Though you are, kind, fooling blue

Eyes kindling wonder and I find
Myself wishing for your
Happiness more often even

Than my own, an odd picture
Of the crest of your back in the back
Of my mind, a sheepish

Smile tremoring the air
Into festive throbs, I think I
Hear *all the bleeding*

Drums, celebration guns and somewhere
You are drinking *guaro*, dark
Plaits of hair striating your already

Reddened face, I search
The pages of a medical encyclopedia
For images, place a diabetic

Within the coils of a *Child-Headed*
Blengin, her hand missing
A finger, the afternoon free

From employment, *every breath*
Death defying, so I go
Nowhere, make too much

Coffee, read a biography of Warhol
Call my dad, bandy
Health insurance, stretch out

On the couch and thrill
At the charge my love's impending
Reach makes, the even plain

Of my chest pale beneath
Its T-shaped turf
Of curly hair and would that bodies

Could rearrange themselves
Like thought, that these gangly
Arms were telescoping

To where you are, the way
My eyes run over
The geography of where you are

To be: *hello.*

The Thirteen-year-old Scream

After work you re-park
The car, head
Over to the Russian hairdresser

For a trim, make small
Talk until "Night Moves" comes
On the radio, then close

Your eyes and tingle
As the razor grazes your now
Pink neck, come home

With the words
Rasping repeatedly, *woke*
Last night to the sound

Of thunder, though you woke
Last night to the thrill
Of naked legs, the air conditioner

Clicking metronomic to the phasings
Of pulse, *what seems*
To happen becomes its own happening

As the truths of a new
Millennium dabble and abscond, each
Consequent possibility—comfort

Nothingness, ecstasy, hope
Mutilation, wonder—occupies
Its provisional realm

Only to misplace itself in the relentless
Shuffle, this morning you gave
Sonny Pain thirty-five cents, Jews

For Jesus gave you
A brochure that asked if you were
Interested in *Computerized*

Donuts and you weren't quite sure
What they were getting
At, the scar on the forearm of

The woman wearing white
Linen pants on
The train was shaped

Like a toy boat on the mottle
Of sewer waves and you proceed to grope
At what can only be approached

By a gape, mouth hot
And dumb, top lip
Thin as the bottom protrudes

In its sensual idiocy and don't you see
The eyes of splendor
Penetrating the face of travail, the interminable

Act of remembering wrongly as *the night*
Takes on a weird electronic
Tingle, for this is the place you return

To through the need
Of living, a cavern translated
By immaterial

White profusions
Like the colors that traffic in the middle
Of clouds beyond the airplane

Window, but here the train shakes
You to sleep until
The stifling obscenity of being

A thing causes the thirteen
Year-old girls to scream
I need a dick in harmonious unison

So that you might
Cringe, so that the transparency
Of grief might blush, so

That the silence might finally fuck off.

A Geometry of Sleeplessness

When I was eight
I knew I would never go
To war and so

I knowingly deformed
My knees in an effort to approximate
My father's, knocked, a little

Awkward, I've never been
One to calmly stomach
The mundane violence of being

A man, nor my own
Coursing veer toward harm, hands
Thick-knuckled and shaky

Even twenty years later, touring
The verdant Bronx
Zoo, I lurk amid *The Land*

Of Darkness, where umbrella-winged fruit
Bats keep pink-eyed
Deer in fear and refuse hate as a kind

Of occupation, though kindness
Is no excuse for simplicity as now it is
Friday and *blood confuses*

The heart, which dithers serenely
One moment only
To be throttled the next, when I was

In high school I used
To keep myself
Up at night envisioning strange

Geometric shapes, each expanding to the point
Where it seemed to miraculously fill
My head and transcend it, this uncanny

Mathematics of volume turning
Spiritual as whole
Hours passed untended, unintended

Fatigue suffusing my days as now
There dwells a plenteousness confiding
Itself by honk and whisper

A squalid transient barking
At pigeon chicks
Hidden behind the psychic's eave

Even now kids hardly want *a mound*
Of clouds to lounge
On, they want their parents' lives

To mean something
More than a fruitless lull
In the maroon

Between existential jokes, my love
Needs sleep, my knees
Need skin and I am becoming too much

A part of this
World, the callus-thick
Feet of a bearded

Bum swelling and bruised like plums
As the heat index touches one
Hundred degrees, *one should not go to church*

If one wants to breathe
Pure air and I now
Know the sum of earnest learning: love

Terrifies the lover and loved alike.

Allegrissimo, or Not as Hell as You

My eyes are no longer cut out
For Midtown, they have slowly grown
Accustomed to roofs and stoops

Suffused by an affable
Dinginess and the textures of low
Sound droning

Without tedium, men call
My dad a man
Of decency, an old

World word, would that each morning
Weren't blooming with limbs, that a kind of
Kind surprise might rupture

The hideous simplicity
Of causation, I writhe at those
That *have contrived*

To retain ignorance, bombastic architects
Of mediocrity, the media's winking
Fingers upon our knees, yet *no one lies so much*

As the indignant and I weep
Only every five years or so, denting
My knuckles on closed

Storefronts as my sense
Of direction daily rearranges
Itself in heat, so I

Take out the fruit
Flies with the garbage
Don my silver

Shorts and dutifully whoosh
Around the park narrowly
Avoiding midday dope smokers' fishing

Poles to visit the recently tagged
White-tipped wallaby as Caribbean
Women push towheaded

Boys in overgrown strollers and *I want*
To always be on film, to be
Caught in the cut coffee sober, to thrill

Allegrissimo in the perseverating
Predawn dash of birds, I applaud the real
Bodies bobbing, collapse

Into the tenderness of leisure and all
My bitter recriminations are sloughed in the line
Between void and voice

Between abyss and abundance, shoplifting
Teenagers spiriting lipstick amid
Half-torn movie tickets, the roots of a once

Stately oak tree sprawled like tentacles
Across the quiet New Jersey
Street, tonight I will play Ping

Pong and drink Negra
Modelo, eye Elisa's budding
Belly and anticipate

Casimir Pulaski Day at the Bowery
Ballroom, for life continues
To astonish, even as the bomb-laden

Few or the bomb-laden
Many wreak fiery remuneration, a light
Skein of cool air descends upon

Brooklyn and the incongruities
Mangle in ways that awe
My ability to reason, which is finally

Unnecessary, as is
My knowledge that beyond it
All *I am*

Not as hell as you.

Dispatches from the Kingdom of No

A hologram is a hologram
Is a hologram, save
For the rapture of a man peddling

Sausages in a black stocking
Cap, unutterable terrors
Encompassing each inch of veritable

Movement into the realm
Of poetry, just as
It is a scandal to live outside

The history of saliva, conjuring
Meek spectacles from the department
Store display windows

The entire globe was surrounded
By quotes, though inside
The bakery an old man quietly

Held a cake emblazoned
With his granddaughter's face
Like Hugo Ball

Restively clutching the 133-year-old skull
Of a 21-year-old girl and wishing
To paint its hollow cheek with kisses

Romancing a corpse
Or simply bargaining with war, atoms
Gripped loosely in the swinging

Of a thick fist, music
Tumbling from the vegetation as if
Today's weather

Were attuned to a Promethean chord
And it is, of
Course, the way the eye

Fixes disaster into art and isn't it
Good to know winter
Is coming, not denying the skylark

Its gradual movement
Toward disintegration? I am
Not like a man

Who says I have never
Been interested in knowing
Knowing and yet

There is sometimes a dark
Companion who pulls, a castanet
Snapping talismanic, calling

The air into mass as in the sea
A dandelion self-disperses and here
On asphalt, a womanly

Hobo strikes at a damp matchbook
Sparks fizzling, I saw myself
Breathing and imagined a tiny tin finger

Rapping at my ribs, today
We saw a mangy parrot voicelessly
Traipse a limb, it's freezing

In Brooklyn and we fear the parrot
Will not survive the night, the moon
Multiplying newness, caressing

Carcasses into alien
Ready-mades and is it right that we
Continue to try to love that part

Of ourselves sampling annihilation?

Being-in-the-Being

If I contain a likeliness
There is no dead
Of night, my immensities gather

Breath around them like bulky nuclei
Harvesting paths, the sun nearly
Always recognizes my hair, the cat

That arises from beneath
The bed is not
Ambivalent and wrongdoing does

Instruct as each particle arrives struck
By an intuition of wholeness, I
Interfere until I can span as enthusiastic

The day as dark, desire to indulge
My feelings unto matter, perhaps to loose
The folds of this waking

Into film as the eye
Cameras through a complex
Act of awareness and *you*

Don't have to wait
Until you die to reconcile the variegated
Guesswork of experience or *question*

The possibility of the question, so
I listen as an unknown
Source of animation kicks a soup

Can down the avenue, myself
Motionlessly appreciating
Its interruptions of clunk, how they penetrate

An otherwise
Dull continuity or work
Themselves neatly

Into dreams, mine nightly full
Of brand names or suspended in an orange
And protracted plummet

From sky to sky or lay
With tigers and sometimes *I sing*
To keep from cursing, braced

By the tedious pangs
Of incarnation, but it wasn't always
This way, I once secreted

My name within the idea
My name became, allowed the magic
Of talk to ricochet

Like a bullet into *the entire*
Future before folding
Itself through its own beginning

As flesh alone dissolves
Any thoughtful stab
At the objective, there is no manner

I wish to absorb
Nor a shape this veering attempts
To conclude, I have dust

To remind me of myself, a church
In California that I hold
In my head and its thick-tongued

Towers toll without
My being there, as my being ebbs only
To erupt in directionless code, I

Was born into The West and the joy
Of unintelligibility or I was
Born into fluorescence and the bloody hands

Of a stranger, the vanishing
Point of my mouth
Exploding into song, proffering

The air with tiny quarrels
Of self, I either writhe
In the baptism of ether or

Soberly find myself
Happening ceaselessly, I tell you
These are just one or two

Of the uncertain occupations
Of *an object in the act*
Of appearing and I scream

It is exhausting to be free.

Toward Perceptual Ensembles

The cat does not avert
Its gaze, it is in
The room whereas I cannot help

But be of, often
Stuck between my wanting
To possess objects

And my responsibility to the objecthood
Of my own watching, so it
Is that my eyes escape me, fleeing

Into the pulse of a summoning
World where there is no
Silence, a night where there is no pitch

Black and I remain
Engaged in *the endless*
Task of expressing

What exists, if my life does not
Explain this
Sentence I think

To let the sentence attempt
To exclaim my life, much as a vulture
Flicked the young da

Vinci's tongue with its tail, I ate inch
Worms for money and wore
My watch on the wrong wrist, even today there

Was a squirrel in Washington
Square Park that brazenly
Did trounce the toes of a studious

Girl in sandals, her pen top
Tossed in terror among
The half-smoked butts, so is it

Any wonder to be subsumed
By the dislocations, to exist as one
Life crossing 16th Street

To overlap the others in tremendous
Inward and oblivious
Leaps, powering the air

With intractable charges, or
Part of the parade of phantasms
Bottlenecking at First

Avenue and Houston, where salamis
Solicit distant gunmen and the retirees
Converge to leer cross-legged

At the exigencies of cinema, even at this
Intersection if I
Tremble my trembling divides

The sleeplessness of others and still
I would not be *a wound in*
The landscape, even had I found quarter from

My engagement with the codes, if *people*
Like to put things in
The ground, I like to fumble

Amid the noise our
Handsome collisions commend
To being, the hopefulness in

Our movement from sleep
To the world when so
Often there is only yourself looking out

As the actor climbs down
From the proscenium to stand beside you
And glare toward the stage in near

Silence as the near darkness falls.

Words lead double lives: anonymously adrift and tethered to author-ship. This book attempts to celebrate both. In addition to those named outright, other voices in the chorus of *American Music* include:

13 and God	Joy Division
Nimer Abderrahman	André Malraux
Gaston Bachelard	Ted Mathys
Jean Michel Basquiat	Maurice Merleau-Ponty
Ingmar Bergman	Mirah
André Breton	Modest Mouse
Built to Spill	Van Morrison
Bill Callahan	Neutral Milk Hotel
Jonathan Cott	Friedrich Nietzsche
Robert Creeley	Will Oldham
Henry Darger	Ron Padgett
Don DeLillo	V.S. Ramachandran
Destroyer	Paul Schilder
Dirty Three	Alexander Scriaban
Ed Dorn	Bob Seger
Marcella Durand	Stars
William Faulkner	Sufjan Stevens
Elizabeth Grosz	Telephone Jim Jesus
Hal Hartley	White Magic
Lyn Hejinian	Why?
Werner Herzog	Bill Withers
I Feel Tractor	

About the Author

Chris Martin's work has appeared in *Jacket, Aufgabe, Lungfull!, Poiesis,* and *Swerve.* He is the editor of *Puppy Flowers,* an online magazine of the arts. After living in Colorado Springs, San Francisco, and St. Paul, he presently resides in Brooklyn. This is his first book.

The Chinese character for poetry is made up of two parts: "word" and "temple." It also serves as pressmark for Copper Canyon Press.

Since 1972, Copper Canyon Press has fostered the work of emerging, established, and world-renowned poets for an expanding audience. The Press thrives with the generous patronage of readers, writers, booksellers, librarians, teachers, students, and funders—everyone who shares the belief that poetry is vital to language and living.

Major funding has been provided by:

Anonymous (2)

Beroz Ferrell & The Point, LLC

Lannan Foundation

National Endowment for the Arts

Cynthia Lovelace Sears and Frank Buxton

Washington State Arts Commission

For information and catalogs:

COPPER CANYON PRESS

Post Office Box 271

Port Townsend, Washington 98368

360-385-4925

www.coppercanyonpress.org

This book is set in Avenir, a geometric sans-serif typeface designed by Adrian Frutiger in 1988. Avenir—the French name for "future"—takes inspiration from early geometric sans-serif typefaces Erbar (1926), designed by Jakob Erbar, and Futura (1927), designed by Paul Renner. Book design and composition by Phil Kovacevich. Printed on archival-quality Glatfelter Author's Text at McNaughton & Gunn, Inc.